GIRLS ROCK!
Newspaper Scoop

Jacqueline Arena

illustrated by
Lloyd Foye

First Published in Great Britain by
RISING STARS UK LTD 2006
22 Grafton Street, London, W1S 4EX

For more information visit our website at:
www.risingstars-uk.com

British Library Cataloguing in Publication Data
A CIP record for this book is available from the British Library.

ISBN: 978-1-84680-059-7

First published in 2006 by
MACMILLAN EDUCATION AUSTRALIA PTY LTD
627 Chapel Street, South Yarra 3141

Visit our website at www.macmillan.com.au or go directly to
www.macmillanlibrary.com.au

Associated companies and representatives throughout the world.

Copyright © Jacqueline Arena, Felice Arena and Phil Kettle 2006

Series created by Felice Arena and Phil Kettle
Project management by Limelight Press Pty Ltd
Cover and text design by Lore Foye
Illustrations by Lloyd Foye
Printed in China

UK Editorial by Westcote Computing Editorial Services

GIRLS ROCK!

Contents

Rachel   Ellie

CHAPTER 1

Write On!

Ellie is in the school playground on her hands and knees pointing a camera at the ground. She has a pad and pencil by her side. Her best friend Rachel runs over to her.

Rachel "Hi Ellie, what are you doing?"

Ellie "I'm looking at these ants."

Rachel "Why?"

Ellie "I've been asked to be a junior
reporter for the school newspaper
and I want to write the best story
ever."

Rachel "Oh, cool. Can I help?"

Ellie gets back up onto her feet.

Ellie "Er, well …"

Rachel "What? I can't help?"

Ellie "It's not that you can't help, it's …"

Rachel "Look Ellie, I know you're a better writer than me, but I can do other things like, er …"

Ellie "I know! You can be my photographer."

Rachel "What? And take photos?"
Ellie "Yes."

Ellie takes off the camera and
hangs it around Rachel's neck.

Rachel "OK, great. I was going to
say I would help you come up with
better stories, but this is cool."
Ellie "Come up with better stories?
What's wrong with writing about all
the different types of ants?"

Rachel "Bor-ing! Major snooze-time! Unless ..."

Ellie "Unless what?"

Rachel "Unless you write about killer ants the size of ponies that march into school and start eating all the desks and chairs in the classrooms."

Ellie "I can't write that! It's not true."

Rachel "But it's more exciting."

Ellie "Yes, but the readers need to know the truth. That's what newspapers are all about."

Rachel "Fine then. If it's a true story you want, I've got the perfect one— and it'll be a really big poop!"

Ellie "You mean 'scoop'. That's a story that no one has ever written about before. Something that will be big news to everyone."

Rachel "Yes, that's right, all of that."

Ellie "So, what's the big scoop?"

Rachel "You'll see. Follow me and I'll lead you to the source."

Ellie "Right, chief. I'm on the case."

CHAPTER 2

Sniffing Out a Story

Ellie follows Rachel across the playground.

Ellie "Rachel, where are we going?"

Rachel "You'll see. This is going to be front page news."

Ellie "I can't wait."

Rachel sneaks up towards the staff room window.

Ellie "Rachel, why are we spying on the teachers?"

Rachel "*Shhh*! Don't let them see us."

Rachel and Ellie hide behind some bushes and peek into the staff room.

Ellie (whispering) "What are we looking at?"

Rachel "There's your big scoop, Ellie."

Ellie takes a closer look at the teachers in the staff room.

Ellie "What scoop? They're just eating and talking."

Rachel "No, look closer!"

Ellie "The only news I can see around here is that Miss Taylor has her hair up today and she usually wears it down."

Rachel "Ellie, how can that be news? That's like saying that birds fly in the sky or polar bears love ice."

Ellie "I suppose so."

Rachel "But it would be huge news if it was something like, birds like to drive sports cars or polar bears love to roller-skate."

Ellie "OK, OK, I understand. So, what's the big scoop?"

Rachel "Look at Mr. Rogers. He's sitting next to Miss Ferrini. And if you look closer, he's holding her hand."

Ellie "So?"

Rachel "Ellie, that's the scoop! Mr. Rogers is in love with Miss Ferrini! Now, if we can only get a picture of them snogging, it'll be front page news!"

Ellie "That's not news. Everyone knows that they're in love. They've been all gooey with each other for ages."

Rachel "They have?"

Ellie "Yes, and they told everyone at assembly last week they're engaged. You were off ill that day."

Ellie gives a sigh then walks off.

Rachel "Where are you going?"
Ellie "To the dinner hall. Maybe I can find a story there."

CHAPTER 3

Spicy Rock Stars

Ellie returns to Rachel after talking to the dinner ladies about some possible story ideas.

Rachel "So, any big news happening there?"

Ellie "Well, they've run out of red apples, but they've still got plenty of green ones."

Rachel "Bor-ing!"

Ellie "What about promoting the yoghurt of the week?"

Rachel "I don't think so!"

Ellie "Or how they've started selling hot and spicy chips."

Rachel "Still bor-ing!"

Ellie "Yes, I know it is."

Rachel "Unless ..."

Ellie "Unless what?"

Rachel "Unless you write about the canteen's hot and spicy apples— how when you bite into them, steam comes out of your ears."

Ellie shakes her head.

Ellie "I want to write about something real, Rachel—like a real reporter."

Rachel "If I were a reporter, I'd want to be a music reporter. I'd interview all the great rock stars. They'd get me up on stage and everyone would be screaming, *'Rachel! Rachel! You're too cool to be a reporter! You should be a rock star and ...'*"

Rachel gets so carried away that she doesn't notice Ellie running off.

Rachel "Now where's she going?"

Ellie heads over towards a group of kids all huddled together. Rachel runs after her.

Rachel "Wait for me, Ellie!"

Rachel catches up with Ellie.

Rachel "What's going on? What's everyone looking at?"

Ellie "That's what I'm trying to find out. Whatever it is, it could be big news."

CHAPTER 4

Secret Agent Squirrel

Ellie and Rachel push themselves
to the front of the group to see what
everyone is looking at.

Rachel "Err, gross!"
Ellie "That's disgusting!"

Everyone is crowded around a dead squirrel. Some of the boys even try to pick it up—until the school caretaker comes and takes it away. Ellie and Rachel go and sit under a tree.

Ellie "I suppose I can write about that."

Rachel "And say what?"

Ellie "That it was an old squirrel and it just died."

Ellie catches Rachel rolling her eyes.

Ellie "I know what you're going to say—bor-ing!"

Rachel "Well, it would be unless ..."

This time Ellie rolls her eyes.

Ellie (sighs) "Unless what?"

Rachel "Unless you write that it was
a secret agent squirrel on a mission
looking for red apples but died of
shock when it saw ..."

Ellie "Rachel!"

Rachel "OK, I'll stop. But what are
you going to write about then?"

CHAPTER 5

The Big Poop ... err, Scoop

Suddenly, a white, wet, gooey drop falls from the branches above on to Ellie's head. Ellie feels her hair with her hand.

Ellie "Err, yuk! A bird just pooped on me!"

Ellie looks up to see a nest full of chicks.

Ellie "I don't believe it. Look, Rachel!"

Rachel "Are they magpie chicks?"

Ellie "No, better. This is huge news! They're owls!"

Rachel "Owls! Wow, that's so cool!"

Ellie "Rachel, can you take a photo?"

Rachel "Sure, how about a close-up?"

Rachel begins to climb the tree.

Ellie "Rachel! What are you doing?
I meant take a photo from here."

But it's too late. Rachel is already
halfway up the tree. She starts
climbing towards the owls' nest.

Ellie "Hey Rachel, can you get a real close-up of the babies? They're so cute, they'll make a great feature!"

Rachel "I'm trying to get out to that branch. If I can get a bit closer, I know I'll get the best shot ever."

Rachel inches her way along the branch.

Ellie "Be careful, Rachel!"

Rachel "I will. Just tell me if you see the mother anywhere. I don't want to be attacked."

Ellie "OK. This is going to be the *best* newspaper story!"

Rachel takes a photo of the owl chicks in their nest. She scampers back down the tree.

Ellie "Tell me what you saw so I can write about it."

Rachel "Well, one was green and slimy. Another one had four eyes and one looked like a lizard with wings."

Ellie "What?"

Rachel "Just joking. They were amazing, Ellie."

Ellie "Give us a look."

Rachel "See, on the screen."

Ellie "Wow! They're amazing! So cute! The story's flooding into my head right now. I have to go to the library and write it all down."

Two days later the school newspaper comes out. Everyone congratulates Ellie and Rachel on a great story.

Ellie "Thanks, Rachel."

Rachel "For what?"

Ellie "For helping me find something exciting to write about."

Rachel "It was nothing. You were the one that ended up getting the big scoop—or is that, the big bird poop?"

GIRLS ROCK!

Rachel

Newspaper Lingo

Ellie

editor The head of a newspaper, the person who decides what stories will appear.

headline The title of a newspaper article. The words are usually short and clever and the letters are in really large print.

paperboy or papergirl A boy or girl who delivers newspapers to people's homes—not paper doll cutouts!

reporter Also called a journalist. They report the news.

scoop The story kind—not the ice cream! A big news story, one that will sell lots of newspapers.

GIRLS ROCK!
Newspaper Must-dos

☆ Know the names of the newspapers in your home town or city. You never know when you might have to say to your friends, "Hey, did you see my photo in the *Times* or the *Gazette* or the *Post*?".

☆ Check out the kids' pull-out section in the newspapers. The weekend papers usually have them. There's plenty of quizzes and cool stuff in these pages—written just for you!

☆ Don't throw out your old newspapers. They can be used for things like wrapping things up or bedding for your dog when she's having puppies.

☆ Read an article from a newspaper and bring it up at the dinner table. Your parents will be really impressed when you say something like, "I read that milk shares are up this week. Dad, you should buy some!"

☆ If you want to be a reporter, grab a pen and pad and interview someone, perhaps your grandparents or teacher. Write a story about them and send it in to your local paper. They might just print it!

☆ Keep a newspaper scrapbook featuring articles and pictures of your favourite things like sports, TV stars or fashion.

GIRLS ROCK!

Newspaper
Instant Info

The oldest weekend newspaper is the *Observer*, published in Britain. Its first issue came out on 4 December, 1791.

On average, the *New York Times* is read by 1,094 000 people from Monday to Friday and by 1,650 000 people on Sundays.

Rupert Murdoch, who was born in Australia, is the managing director of many newspapers including the *New York Post* (United States) and the *Sun* (UK).

One of the biggest selling newspapers in Britain is the *News of the World*.

Lists of best-selling books are featured in many newspapers. One of the most famous lists is the *New York Times' Bestseller List*.

Most sports news is featured in the back pages of a newspaper.

Clark Kent, better known as Superman, worked as a reporter for a newspaper called the *Daily Planet*.

There are over 10,000 newspapers available on the Internet. Now that's saving paper!

Think Tank

1 Which superhero worked as a reporter on a daily newspaper?

2 What's a newspaper scoop?

3 Who decides what stories will appear in a newspaper?

4 Where can you read news stories without looking at paper?

5 What's a headline?

6 Name some things you can do with newspaper when you are not reading it?

7 Who delivers newspapers to homes, usually early in the morning?

8 Where is the sports section found in most newspapers?

Answers

1 Superman worked as a reporter on the *Daily Planet*.

2 A newspaper scoop is big and breaking news, something that no one has ever reported before.

3 The editor decides what stories will appear in a newspaper. The editor is the boss!

4 You can read paperless news stories on the Internet.

5 A headline is the main title of a newspaper story.

6 You can use newspaper for lots of things like wrapping things up, and lining your dog's basket when she is ready to have puppies. Add your own ideas—all answers are correct!

7 Paperboys or papergirls deliver papers to homes.

8 The sports section is usually found at the back of most newspapers.

How did you score?

- If you got all 8 questions correct, you should consider being a reporter for your school newspaper. Try reading a newspaper article every day—you'll probably love it!

- If you got 6 questions correct, then you don't mind reading a newspaper, but only the kids' pull-out section.

- If you got fewer than 4 questions correct, then you love newspapers—but only to line the bottom of your budgie's cage!

Hey Girls!

I hope that you have as much fun reading my story as I have had writing it. I loved reading and writing stories when I was young.

Here are some suggestions that might help you enjoy reading even more than you do now.

At school, why don't you use "Newspaper Scoop" as a play and you and your friends can be the actors. Get some old newspapers, a pad, a pencil and a camera to use as props. So ... have you decided who is going to be Ellie and who is going to be Rachel? And what about the narrator?

Now act out the story in front of your friends. I'm sure you'll have a great time!

You also might like to take this story home and get someone in your family to read it with you. Maybe they can take on a part in the story.

Whatever you choose to do, you can have as much fun with reading and writing as a polar bear in a freezer!

And remember, Girls Rock!

Jacqueline Soena

GIRLS ROCK!

When We Were Kids

Jacqueline

Shey

Jacqueline talked to Shey, another *Girls Rock!* author

Jacqueline "Have you ever been in the newspaper?"

Shey "Yes, when I was younger."

Jacqueline "Cool. It must have have been exciting to see yourself in print."

Shey "Well, it was for Mum and Dad. Everyone said I looked great."

Jacqueline "So why weren't you excited?"

Shey "Because I was busy gurgling."

Jacqueline "Gurgling?"

Shey "Yes, it was a photo of me on the day I was born!"

What a Laugh!

Q What books do owls like?

A Hoot-dunnits!

GIRLS ROCK!

The Sleepover

Pool Pals

Bowling Buddies

Girl Pirates

Netball Showdown

School Play Stars

Diary Disaster

Horsing Around

Newspaper Scoop

Snowball Attack

Dog on the Loose

Escalator Escapade

Cooking Catastrophe

Talent Quest

Wild Ride

Camping Chaos

Mummy Mania

Skater Chicks

GIRLS ROCK! books are available from most booksellers. For mail order information please call Rising Stars on 0870 40 20 40 8 or visit www.risingstars-uk.com

44